Luna

and
the Well of Secrets

J. H. Sweet

Illustrated by Tara Larsen Chang

SOURCEBOOKS
Jabberwocky
AN IMPRINT OF SOURCEBOOKS

Published by Sourcebooks Jabberwocky, an imprint of
Sourcebooks, Inc.
P.O. Box 4410, Naperville, Illinois 60567-4410
(630) 961-3900
Fax: (630) 961-2168
www.sourcebooks.com

Library of Congress Cataloging-in-Publication Data

Sweet, J. H.
   Luna and the Well of Secrets / J. H. Sweet ; [illustrations by Tara
Larsen Chang].
      p. cm. — (The Fairy Chronicles ; bk. 10)
   Summary: When fairies begin disappearing from around the globe,
Luna and her fairy friends are assigned to travel to the Well of
Secrets and with their combined strengths try to rescue them.
   ISBN-13: 978-1-4022-1164-5 (pbk. : alk. paper)
   ISBN-10: 1-4022-1164-3 (pbk. : alk. paper) [1. Fairies—Fiction. 2.
Magic—Fiction. 3. Cooperativeness—Fiction.] I. Chang, Tara Larsen,
ill. II. Title.

PZ7.S9547Lu 2008
[Fic]—dc22
                                        2007044115

              Printed and bound in China
              IM 10 9 8 7 6 5 4 3 2 1

To the heroes of the world,
however great, however small

MEET THE

Luna

NAME:
Hope Valdez

FAIRY NAME AND SPIRIT:
Luna

WAND:
Single Thorn from Prickly
Pear Cactus

GIFT:
Strength, endurance, and
ability to perform magic
without a wand

MENTOR:
Amelia Thompson,
Madam Finch

Snapdragon

NAME:
Bettina Gregory

FAIRY NAME AND SPIRIT:
Snapdragon

WAND:
Spiral-Shaped Black
Boar Bristle

GIFT:
Fierceness and speed

MENTOR:
Mrs. Renquist,
Madam Swallowtail

FAIRY TEAM

Firefly

Primrose

NAME:	NAME:
Lenox Hart	Taylor Buchanan
FAIRY NAME AND SPIRIT:	FAIRY NAME AND SPIRIT:
Firefly	Primrose
WAND:	WAND:
Single Piece of Straw	Small, Black Raven Feather
GIFT:	GIFT:
A great light within	Ability to solve mysteries
MENTOR:	MENTOR:
Mrs. Pelter,	Mrs. Renquist,
Madam June Beetle	Madam Swallowtail

Inside you is the power to do anything™

The Fairy Chronicles

Come visit us at fairychronicles.com

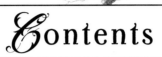

$\mathscr{C}$ontents

Chapter One

Luna

Two days after Christmas, the weather had finally turned cold. It wasn't at all odd to be seventy degrees in December in South Texas, but days in the forties were welcomed by those who liked cooler Christmastimes.

This Christmas vacation had been the best ever for Hope Valdez. Just before Christmas, she had gone on an exciting adventure with several of her friends that had included meeting a gremlin, a dwarf, a gargoyle, and a magical spirit known as the Wishmaker.

It might seem strange for ordinary young girls to have contact with magical creatures, but Hope and her friends were also fairies. And the job of fairies was to protect nature and fix problems, mainly problems caused by other magical creatures. So Hope and her fellow fairies stayed very busy year round.

Fairy activities had to be kept secret from non-magical people because many of them did not believe in fairies, and those who did would not likely be able to understand the need for young girls to be off on dangerous fairy missions sometimes.

Regular people could not even recognize fairies when they saw them. To non-magical people, fairies only appeared to look like their fairy spirits such as flowers, tiny sea creatures, butterflies, tree blossoms, berries, fireflies, small animals, birds, and the like. Being seen was only tricky when people happened to spot fairies at a time of year when certain flowers or insects were out of season.

Hope was a luna moth fairy. In the standard fairy form of six inches, Luna had large, pale green, glowing wings; and she wore a misty green, velvety dress with slippers to match. Her wings had a soft pink edge, a long curving tail, and enormous luminous eyespots. Luna also had straight dark hair that came to just below her shoulders. In the belt of her dress, she carried a small pouch of pixie dust, the fairy handbook, and her wand.

Luna's wand was a single thorn from a prickly pear cactus. It was long, sharp like a needle, and gleaming white. But there was something extremely significant about the thorn: Luna never used it and never needed to. She was the only fairy in existence who did not need a wand to perform magic. She still carried her wand, out of sentiment, but the cactus thorn was in a perpetual state of rest.

Each fairy was given a unique gift that was kind of like a specialty. Like all butterfly and moth fairies, Luna had strength and endurance as gifts. She also had extremely keen eyesight. Not only was she able to see things at great distances; but also, she was able to see things clearly for what they really were. She was not easily deceived by appearances, since things were not always as they seemed to be.

Madam Finch was Luna's mentor. Mentors were usually older fairies who supervised the younger ones. Luna had learned she was a fairy at age eight. When it was discovered that she did not need a wand to perform fairy magic, Madam Finch discussed the issue with Madam Toad, the leader of the fairies for the Southwest region. They agreed that Luna was probably one of the most powerful fairies ever created, and that her ability to perform magic without a wand was an extra fairy gift.

Since Luna was still young, at age nine, and because she had incredibly powerful fairy gifts, Madam Finch watched her closely. But Luna was already proving to be very careful and trustworthy. Young fairies were not allowed to use their powers lightly. Fairy magic and gifts were not supposed to be used for trivial matters or to solve everyday problems. In fact, younger fairies needed approval from their mentors to perform magic at all.

Luna was very true to the Fairy Code of Conduct and strictly followed the rules. She also knew even without being told that she was an extremely powerful fairy. This made her very determined to always use her gifts to contribute something good to the world, and never inappropriately.

Madam Finch had blond hair, and her real name was Mrs. Thompson. She was a ballet instructor and a Girls Club sponsor. This gave her the ability to spend a lot of time mentoring young fairies and providing good excuses for them to spend time away from home while engaged in fairy activities. As a fairy, Madam Finch wore a greenish-yellow dress made of tiny finch feathers that came almost to her ankles. She had feathery green wings and carried a tiger whisker wand.

Two of Luna's fairy friends, Bettina Gregory and Taylor Buchanan, were coming over for the afternoon to visit.

Bettina had been given the fairy spirit of a snapdragon flower. In fairy form, she wore a yellow and orange dress made of furled snapdragon petals; and her bright orange wings were very tall and wispy. She also had short brown hair and carried a wand made of a black boar bristle that was spiraled like a corkscrew. Her special fairy gift was a fierce

Madam Finch

ability to defend, protect, and even attack, if necessary. Snapdragon could also fly very fast, like a speedy dragon. The snapdragon flower was named because of its resemblance to the mouth of a dragon, and the snapdragon fairy spirit was gifted with fierce dragon qualities, both offensive and defensive.

Taylor's fairy spirit was that of an evening primrose, a common spring wildflower in Texas. Primrose wore a pale pink dress made of translucent flower petals with delicate gold veins, and her tiny wings were a soft gold color. Her hair was blond and wavy, and she carried a raven feather for her wand. Primrose's special fairy gift was the ability to pick up on small details and solve mysteries. This had proven very helpful just before Christmas. She was able to solve the mystery of what the gremlin, gargoyle, and dwarf all had in common, which then led to the

discovery of the Wishmaker. Primrose also had great energy after dark because primrose flowers most often opened up, springing to life, in the evenings.

The girls drank hot chocolate while they sat on the rug in Hope's room and listened to stories about Christmases in Mexico. Hope had lived with her grandparents in Mexico when she was very young. She spoke both English and Spanish, and knew a lot about her heritage. The other girls loved hearing about the colorful customs and traditions of Mexico. It was fun to learn about festivals and celebrations in other countries. Hope was very good at describing these things, so her friends could almost imagine that they were there.

While they were talking, Mrs. Valdez brought in a large plate of penuche, which was a kind of yummy brown sugar fudge, for the girls to have with their hot chocolate.

When the doorbell rang a little while later, they went to investigate.

Mrs. Thompson was talking with Mr. and Mrs. Valdez in the living room. The girls knew that this unexpected visit must have something to do with important fairy business. They kept silent, while the fairy mentor expertly and quickly convinced Hope's parents that she needed to take Hope, Bettina, and Taylor to an impromptu Girls Club activity. She also cleverly arranged for a sleepover at her house that night.

With permission from her parents, Luna hastily packed a small bag with pajamas, clean clothes, and her hairbrush and toothbrush.

Mrs. Thompson had already arranged for time away from home with the parents of both Snapdragon and Primrose. She had explained that the Girls Club event involved important holiday charity work that needed to be done right away, and that the girls wouldn't have time for very many of these activities after school started again.

Mrs. Thompson never had much trouble arranging these kinds of things. It was often nice for parents to hand over responsibility to someone else for a while and take a break from very energetic young girls.

Chapter Two

The Mission

There was no time to plan for a traditional Fairy Circle. Instead, Madam Finch drove Luna, Primrose, and Snapdragon to Madam Toad's house on Belvin Street.

Madam Toad's real name was Mrs. Jenkins; and her house was a large, white, three-story historic home. They met in her parlor. Madam Toad had readied tea and cookies for them, but everyone was too nervous about the unknown purpose of the meeting to eat or drink anything.

Another fairy was already there. Firefly was a little older than the other girls. Her real name was Lenox Hart. Firefly had led a quest this past spring, with a black squirrel, to find the Black Stag and magical blue moon clover. She had helped to save all creatures, including mankind, from an evil goblin curse. The younger fairies all looked up to Firefly and admired her very much.

Firefly was a golden brown fairy with bright gold wings and a silky brown dress. She had straight auburn hair and carried a single piece of gleaming straw for her wand. Her special fairy gift was a light greater than any other fairy. It helped to light dark places and served as a guide for her. Because her light could act as a warning, Firefly was seldom misled by evil spirits.

Madam Robin was also present at the meeting. She too was a fairy mentor, but Madam Robin was unique in the realm of fairies because she was not a fairy. She was actually a robin that had been bewitched with the gift of speech and long life. Madam Robin was very mysterious to the younger fairies because no one seemed to know the story of how, when, or why she had been enchanted. No one knew how old she was, just that she was wise and beautiful, and a very good fairy mentor.

Madam Toad had set out a plate of birdseed and a dish of water for Madam Robin, but they also remained untouched because Madam Robin was too troubled to eat or drink.

The fairy leader got down to business quickly. "Luna, you have been selected to lead a very important mission. Snapdragon, Firefly, and Primrose will accompany you; and Madam Finch will supervise." Madam Toad took a deep breath, then added, "Three bat fairies have been abducted."

The young fairies all looked at each other, startled. None of them had ever met a bat fairy before. They listened carefully as Madam Toad explained further. "On Christmas day, a pipistrelle bat fairy from Great Britain, a bumblebee bat fairy from Thailand, and a spotted bat fairy from down near the border of Texas and Mexico were all kidnapped.

"There must be extremely powerful magic involved to snatch fairies from three completely different parts of the world all in one day." Madam Toad's face wore a puzzled expression as she continued. "And the reason only bat fairies were taken is unknown. We have received reports from bird observers that the fairies were taken into the Well of Secrets."

Madam Toad paused for a moment before she went on. "I won't tell you here what secrets the well contains.

We cannot take a chance of being overheard. Madam Finch will explain to you about the purpose of the well when you arrive at your destination.

"Also, the secrets of the well must be kept as secrets. That is very important. I am instructing you now, not even to share the information with other fairies upon your return. The fewer people who know about the well, and its location and purpose, the better."

The young fairies all nodded solemnly.

Madam Toad then finished giving her instructions. "An eagle is waiting outside to take you to the well. This may be the most dangerous fairy mission ever. I send you on it very reluctantly, but we must try to help recover the bat fairies. I fear a dark fate awaits them. If they are not rescued quickly, they will likely experience a lifetime of terrible torment and misery."

Provisions had already been packed in little backpacks and included water, raspberries, peanut butter and marshmallow crème sandwiches, and lemon jellybeans.

Luna, Snapdragon, Primrose, Firefly, and Madam Finch all trooped quickly out into the yard to the waiting eagle. The bird knew exactly where to go. As soon as the five fairies had landed on his back, he took off. Rising swiftly, the eagle headed east.

As Madam Toad and Madam Robin watched them go, they looked worriedly at one another.

"You have selected the right fairies for the mission," said Madam Robin, quietly. "I am sure of it."

"But I'm not sure if it was correct not to warn them of what they may be facing, if the rumor is true," said Madam Toad. There was an unsteady waver in her voice

that no fairy had ever heard from their leader before.

Madam Robin was glad that she was the only one to witness Madam Toad's struggle with her decision to send the fairies on a mission without full information. She hurried to reassure Madam Toad that she had made a good choice. "It is better that they don't have any preformed opinions. They will be stronger if they are able to judge for themselves based on the actual situation. Our ideas and input may not be accurate, since we are not there to see for ourselves."

Madam Robin paused for a moment, then added, "I myself do not believe the rumor. I have known her for over thirty years. I cannot believe that she has given in after all this time. I will never believe her capable of this."

Madam Toad nodded, and said, "You are right. They must see everything for

themselves in order to make the right decisions and be successful." Again nodding, she added, "Our opinions might have clouded their judgment. Too much inform- ation is not always a good thing. We could have ruined the mission by forewarning them."

Chapter Three

Eventide, the Land of Darkness

After two hours of flight, the eagle dropped the fairies off on the shore of a small inlet bay that was part of a gigantic lake. The fairies thanked the eagle, and he nodded to them as he quickly departed. No birds ever approached the Well of Secrets closely, if they could help it. The shore of the bay, near a path to the well, was as close as the eagle dared to come. This was fine with the fairies because Madam Finch needed to explain a few things before they made their way down the path.

However, before she could begin speaking, the fairies were distracted by a vast number of freshwater merfolk in the shallows of the bay. "Hello! Hello!" they called. "Come, follow us! Do not go inland! Come away! Come away with us!" There were about twenty-five merfolk in all, waving to the fairies while splashing and diving about.

The tails of both the mermen and merwomen were a sparkling, deep blue color. The merpeople also had dark green fins and long green hair that looked like curled seaweed strands. As they dove and swam, they flashed brilliantly in the afternoon sunshine, glinting brightly and holding the attention of the mesmerized fairies. None of the younger fairies had ever seen merfolk before, and they never dreamed they would see so many at once.

Telling the girls to stay put and wait for her, Madam Finch quickly flew out to speak to them. She conversed with the merfolk for some time. When the fairy mentor returned to the shore, the merpeople began swimming away, but they glanced worriedly over their shoulders as they departed.

As she arrived back on shore, Madam Finch told the girls, "The merpeople have the task of distracting others away from the path to the Well of Secrets. It is their job to lead creatures of all kinds in another direction."

Madam Finch sighed, thinking carefully for a few moments before continuing. Finally, she said, "The Well of Secrets contains great evil. It is the doorway to a place called Eventide, the Land of Darkness. The name Eventide is very deceptive. It is a poetic name that is very alluring. The word itself means evening. But in truth, Eventide, in this case, means approaching darkness and coming doom.

The Land of Darkness is a storage place for evil, and the Well of Secrets is sealed by spells to contain that evil.

"The Demon of Darkness makes his home in Eventide," Madam Finch added. "I hope we can recover the bat fairies without having to face him. He is not terribly powerful himself, because it is more the fear of darkness that is potent. However, when the demon works his way into the hearts and minds of others, he can wield great power through them. His corruption causes tremendously dark actions and events. It is believed that the Demon of Darkness has evil witches working for him."

Next, Madam Finch pointed to a spot behind them where two, dead-looking trees with ugly black trunks grew. "That spot marks the beginning of the path to the well," she said. "We must stay close together. Remember, we are strongest as a group. Try not to get separated at all on this mission."

Before departing to seek the well, the fairies ate a quick meal of raspberries and peanut butter and marshmallow crème sandwiches to keep their strength up. They would need energy to face darkness and evil. Then, flying very closely together, they began the trek down the dark path winding through the trees.

The fairies reached the end of the path fairly quickly. The ancient well sat in a small, perfectly circular clearing surrounded by barren ground with only a bit of yellow and brown winter grasses growing around the edges. Many ugly dead trees stood at the fringes of the clearing. The few living trees mixed in were leaning backwards, and looked as though they were afraid to grow too near the well.

The mouth of the Well of Secrets was round, about four feet high, and was

made of old gray stones. As the fairies approached, they held back a little. A coldness and chill surrounded them, making them shiver.

Luna knew what she had to do as leader of this mission. She flew to the opening and hovered over the dark hole, peering intently into the abyss. "There is no water," she announced. "I can only see the ground very far below." Luna's wings were glowing softly. Next, she spoke to Firefly. "Follow directly behind me to help light the way."

Firefly nodded and took up position as instructed. The other fairies all followed suit and stayed as closely together as possible as they entered the Well of Secrets.

Inside, the cold was very intense. They could feel no wind, just icy cold and complete calm. Even their wings didn't generate any breeze in the stillness. It was as though that type of movement was being sucked into the darkness.

Firefly glowed brightly, helping to keep their spirits up with her intense light. And Primrose and Snapdragon lit their wands with quiet whispers of "*Fairy light.*" The tips of the raven feather and boar bristle glowed softly in the growing blackness.

The trip to the bottom of the well took a long time. And the downward journey made the fairies feel almost as though they were falling, even though they had perfect control over their wings and the rate of their descent.

As they traveled, the fairies noticed that some of the bricks in the walls of the well were slightly different colors and stood out from the surrounding gray stones. A few of the strangely colored bricks shimmered softly as though a light of some sort was hidden within them. When they passed a pale blue brick, the fairies thought they smelled fresh laundry. At one point, directly in front of a glowing red brick, they all became very drowsy. But the sleepiness soon passed as they continued their downward journey. When they finally reached the bottom, they breathed a sigh of relief, even though they feared what they might find.

The bottom of the well was open, and the ground upon which the fairies landed was about ten feet from the round stone bottom of the well. Glancing upwards, the fairies could see that the underside of the well looked just like the entrance at the top, but upside down. They were very happy that the opening didn't just magically disappear or hide itself. It was comforting to see a way out of Eventide.

The Land of Darkness was very flat and a stormy gray color as far as they could see.

There was no vegetation, except for a few dead-looking, craggy trees dotting the landscape. In the distance, the fairies viewed a large black lake. There was something strange about the lake; the water was almost too still and smooth, like an immense black mirror.

Overhead, the sky was the same cloudy gray color as the ground; and the distant horizon was not even noticeable, since the colors of the sky and earth blended together so perfectly. There was no evidence of stars, sun, or moon, even though the landscape was visible by some source of light. The only observable light source was the fairies and their wands.

Just beyond the far shore of the lake, Luna saw several huge creatures around the size of ogres, maybe fifteen feet or taller. They looked sort of like elephants standing on their back legs. The creatures were gray in color with long noses and big, elephant-like, floppy ears. But they had webbed hands and feet, and were covered all over in large, lizardy scales.

With long sharp sticks, the lizard-like elephant monsters were poking and prodding a group of smaller creatures. Luna could see several of the scaly giants halfway submerged in the black lake, while the others milled about on the shore.

The monsters were gorfenklugs, servants of the Demon of Darkness, and only existed in Eventide. They acted as wardens and slave masters for the beings the demon had captured and imprisoned over the years.

With her excellent eyesight, Luna could see the gorfenklugs clearly, but she could not make out the smaller creatures they were herding. She didn't mention what she saw to her fellow fairies. They were all already frightened enough. The sight of the huge, cruel-looking beasts terrified Luna, but she didn't want to pass on any extra reason for her friends to fear their surroundings. She hoped the monsters would stay well away from them.

Behind the fairies sat a large pavilion made of light gray stone. Still staying very close together, the group made their way toward the structure.

The pavilion was dark inside, just like the landscape, and had huge stone columns spaced every few feet to hold up the roof. A grand piano sat in one corner of the structure. Another corner was filled with a huge marble pedestal upon which sat an oversized mirror. The mirror was the size of a large painting and was tilted on an easel back. A massive stone table and chairs occupied the center of the enclosure. On the table, trapped in a box that looked as though it

were made of greenish-gold light, were the three bat fairies.

The bumblebee bat fairy was slightly smaller than the other two. She had tiny, pale gray wings and a soft, furry brown dress with a patch of white on the front. The pipistrelle bat fairy was a darker color with tall brown wings. Her shiny fur dress was a deep, chocolate-brown color with just a bit of light brown streaking down the front. The spotted bat fairy had pale pink wings and wore a black fur dress marked with three white spots—one on each shoulder and one in the middle of her back. Her dress also had a high, white fur collar that looked like a muff.

The bat fairies looked very tired, and evidently could not speak. They gestured to the other fairies but could not make themselves understood. With much pointing, waving, and signaling, the three fairies seemed to be warning the newcomers to

leave. However, this was a rescue mission, and the newly arrived fairies had no intention of leaving the three bat fairies trapped in a box of light in the Land of Darkness.

As the rescuers hovered beside the box, the bat fairies pointed frantically to the mirror and the piano; but again, they could not make themselves understood through their motions.

Luna slowly approached the mirror, her fellow fairies following closely. This was not an ordinary looking glass. The fairies' reflections were faintly visible, but they could see another person inside the glass.

The occupant of the mirror was a young woman who was fast asleep on a dark green couch in a small room. She had straight dark hair pulled into a ponytail, and was dressed entirely in black with a close-fitting sweater and knit pants. The sweater had long sleeves and a high turtle-neck. She also wore short black boots.

A sinister presence seemed to surround the sleeping figure. The woman's expression was quite calm, but there was something about the room, the couch, and the sleep that was unnatural, disturbing, and very mysterious.

Luna cautiously knocked on the glassy surface of the mirror. She wasn't sure if it was a good idea or not to try to wake the sleeping woman, but she couldn't think of anything else to do. However, the knocking had no effect. The woman slept on.

Chapter Four

The Light Witch

The fairies slowly made their way back to the table and the box of light. Landing next to the trapped fairies, they discussed various spells, but no one could figure out a spell that would release the bat fairies.

The box felt like a solid object when touched. Luna was vaguely wondering if it could be safely broken somehow, when the fairies were distracted by a beautiful figure in white approaching the pavilion.

The approaching figure was a delicate woman with long, silvery-blond hair and pale skin. She was dressed in brilliant white with a long-sleeved sheer blouse, flowing silk pants, and pearly white slippers. "Hello!" she called to them. "I am so glad you have come. Perhaps you can help me free the bat fairies."

As the woman entered the pavilion, the fairies slowly approached her. She introduced herself as they drew near. "I am known as the Light Witch, and I usually live in your world. I entered the doorway to Eventide when it became known to me that the Dark Witch had taken several fairies into the Well of Secrets."

The Light Witch sounded concerned as she went on. "The Dark Witch works for the Demon of Darkness, and she is very evil. In fact, she is the most powerful Dark Witch born in a century. I was able to use a spell to trap her in the mirror, but she is very strong. I have battled her for many years and have never found a way to defeat her. Unfortunately, I have been unable to break the spell she used to imprison the fairies in the box of light."

Although the Light Witch was bright and beautiful, there was something cold and sinister growing in the air around the pavilion. The fairies all hovered very close together for protection from this cold. Unfortunately, there was none, and they began shivering uncontrollably.

"Be very careful not to touch the piano," the Light Witch told them. "Playing a certain combination of keys would release the Dark Witch from the spell that keeps her contained in the mirror."

Luna and her friends noticed that the bat fairies had once more begun gesturing frantically and wildly to them; but again, their waving and pointing made no sense.

"Why *d*-id she *t-t*-take bat fairies?" asked Luna, her teeth chattering.

the Light Witch

"There is a legend that bat fairies are the most powerful of all fairies," answered the Light Witch.

"I have never heard that," said Madam Finch. "And I don't think it is true, though I admit that I do not know any bat fairies personally."

The Light Witch responded. "The Dark Witch believes the legend. She captured the fairies with dark magic and was planning to try to convert them to darkness, to serve evil and work for the Demon of Darkness to carry out his dark plans.

"I must warn you," the Light Witch added. "The spell trapping the Dark Witch in the mirror can barely contain her force." The Light Witch approached the mirror as she continued her warning. "She is able to wake every twelve hours for twelve minutes only. During those times, I watch her very carefully to prevent her escape. The time is fast approaching for her to wake."

The Light Witch's voice was a bit strained as she went on. "The Dark Witch is extremely cunning and clever. She will tell lies. Do not believe anything she says. She can bewitch creatures of all kinds with a single look, and sometimes with just the sound of her voice."

The hovering group of fairies was very uneasy, in addition to being extremely cold. It wasn't just the words of warning from the Light Witch. There was something unspeakable and menacing in the air, closing in around them.

Firefly's shivering had become intense shuddering. "S-s-something is t-terribly wrong!" she cried desperately.

The Light Witch spoke kindly to her. "You are in the Land of Darkness; you are bound to feel very unsettled."

But Firefly shook her head, trembling. "S-something else is wrong."

the DarkWitch

The other fairies all trusted their friend's instinct and looked warily around them.

Primrose voiced her feelings too. "There is *s-s*-something *v*-very mysterious and wrong here, but I can't *p*-pinpoint what it is."

Again the Light Witch spoke reassuringly. "You are probably feeling the approach of the waking of the Dark Witch. She is tremendously evil and terribly powerful. Remember, do not believe anything she says. She will tell lies that sound like the truth."

The fairies all stared with horror into the mirror as the figure of the Dark Witch began to stir.

$\mathscr{C}$aptured

$\mathscr{I}$nside the looking glass, the Dark Witch rose from the green couch. She made her way quickly to the mirror's surface, looked out, and calmly surveyed the scene and the newcomers. Her eyes rested briefly on the three bat fairies with a concerned look, as though she were checking to make sure they were still contained in the box of light. Then she stared intently for a moment at the Light Witch. Finally, she turned her attention to the newly arrived fairies, looking closely at them. She made eye contact with each of them in turn, but did not speak. A brief smile touched her lips as her penetrating gaze met Luna's dark brown eyes. They stared at each other for a long while. The Dark Witch's eyes were intense, alive, and confident, while Luna's were searching and questioning.

Finally, the Dark Witch spoke, and her words were careful and slow. She addressed the Light Witch first. "You can live a lie, but you cannot conceal one forever." Then, turning to the fairies, the Dark Witch spoke directly to Luna. "Do not trust what you see. Appearances can be very deceiving. Things are not what they seem."

The voice of the Dark Witch was very comforting and warming, and it seemed to drive away some of the chill from the air in the pavilion.

"Be careful!" cried the Light Witch. "She is trying to bewitch you. Remember how powerful she is!" The voice of the Light Witch was like an icy blast.

Almost immediately, Firefly shouted to her friends. "We are being misled! We have nothing to fear from the Dark Witch! I am sure of it!"

The Light Witch raised her hands, just as Luna and Snapdragon tried to move in front of the other fairies. Unfortunately, they were not fast enough to defend themselves.

With a quick swipe of one hand, the Light Witch caused all of the fairies' wands to zoom towards her, as though she were holding a powerful wand magnet. Then, with a quick flick of her finger, the Light Witch conjured up a box of light identical to the one that imprisoned the bat fairies. The box was evidently something like a high-powered vacuum. Before they even had a chance to struggle, the fairies were sucked into the box by a terrific force.

The Light Witch smiled smugly and evilly as she carried the box to the table, setting it beside the bat fairies' box. "That was almost too easy," she said.

As the Light Witch stared coldly at the fairies, she added, "So much for fearing fairy power. Perhaps fairies would not be as useful as I had hoped in working for the Demon of Darkness. Fairy magic is obviously nothing compared to witch magic."

Slipping the fairies' wands into her blouse pocket, the Light Witch approached the mirror. "Go back to sleep!" she hissed at the Dark Witch. "Eventually, you will starve to death in there, and I will never again have to worry about dealing with you."

Primrose said sadly to her friends, "Well, there is no longer anything mysterious here. We have been deceived."

Snapdragon was pacing and stomping around, furious with herself. "What good am I on this mission?" she spat. "I wasn't fast enough, or fierce enough, to prevent this!"

"No!" commanded Madam Finch. "Stop that thinking at once! You cannot physically fight magic this powerful. We need to stay calm and start using our heads."

Their supervisor's words reassured the young fairies, and they began brainstorming to try to find a solution.

"I wonder if any of the bat fairies know sign language," said Primrose. She was fluent in American Sign Language because her cousin was deaf. In fact, all of the fairies in the Southwest region knew some sign language because Primrose's cousin was also a fairy—a blue hollyhock fairy. Many of the fairies were taking sign language classes at the local community college.

"It wouldn't matter if they know sign language," said Firefly, "unless the spotted bat fairy does, because other

53

countries have their own versions of sign language."

Primrose sighed. "Oh, that's right."

"But it was a good thought," said Luna. "Let's keep trying to come up with a plan. Don't pay any attention to what the Light Witch said. We are very powerful. We were just deceived." As she spoke, Luna ran her hands along the inner walls of their prison. The surface of glowing light felt very hard, like thick glass.

Inside their box, the bat fairies were extremely exhausted. They sat huddled together sadly. The Light Witch was trying to starve them too, just as she was doing to the Dark Witch. The kidnapped fairies had shared a small container of water that the pipistrelle bat fairy had with her when they were captured. But they had run out this morning, and they had had no food for two days. The Light Witch had used a spell to take away their speech. And they were very sad that they had been unable to warn the other fairies about the Light Witch. At this point, they were almost out of hope.

However, Hope, as Luna, was not giving up. In fact, she was getting ready to act. But she was being very careful; she didn't want to fail. So she would delay just long enough to think everything through to ensure that her actions would be successful.

The Dark Witch gave a last look of concern at the fairies before she drifted off to sleep again when her twelve waking minutes ended.

Chapter Six

*E*scape from the Mirror

en minutes later, the fairies were still brainstorming, but no one had any good ideas yet. Luna was still thinking her private plan through. She didn't want to put anyone in danger by acting too quickly, and she knew the others would not be able to help her since they didn't have their wands.

The Light Witch came to sit in one of the chairs at the stone table. Watching the fairies, and sneering at them, she privately congratulated herself on successfully capturing the Dark Witch and eight fairies. The gloating look on her face was sickening.

Suddenly, an elf owl flew into the pavilion, landing next to the fairies in their boxes of light. The elf owl was very tiny and could have fit easily into the palm of a person's hand. He had soft, brownish-gray feathers with a few cinnamon speckles and spots on his head and wings.

The Light Witch acted as quickly as before. "Oh no you don't!" she cried angrily. "You won't get the chance to help her!" And with a quick flick of her finger, the tiny elf owl was imprisoned in yet another box of light.

However, enraged as she was at the arrival of the bird, and feeling very good about her number of captures, the Light Witch had overlooked one thing. A tiny ladybug had traveled in with the elf owl, perched on his head. And just before the Light Witch enclosed the tiny bird in the box of light, the ladybug took off from the owl's head and flew to the mirror.

The fairies watched, but the Light Witch took no notice. She stood gloating over the elf owl's box with an ugly smirk on her face. Either she didn't see the tiny ladybug, or she didn't think there could be any danger from something that small.

The ladybug stayed for only a fraction of a second on the surface of the mirror, then she quickly flew to the piano. At the moment she reached the instrument, the ladybug transformed into the most beautiful creature the fairies had ever seen.

The ladybug was not a ladybug after all. She was a sphilox, an elf fairy of light with the ability to change shapes. The fairies had heard of sphiloxes before, but none of them had ever seen one. The sphilox was about the size of a large walnut and was made entirely of light. Her tiny wings were fluttering as fast as a hummingbird's, and her body was very delicate and spindly.

Very quickly, the sphilox's spidery limbs touched several black keys of the piano in a specific order, to play the tune that would release the Dark Witch from the mirror. As the notes were played, an eerie, deep sounding music issued from the instrument. Completely taken by surprise, the Light Witch whirled quickly from the table and ran toward the mirror, just as the Dark Witch was climbing out of it.

Unfortunately, the Dark Witch was weak from her imprisonment, just like the bat fairies. The Light Witch raised her hand and with only a slight wave was able to throw the Dark Witch halfway across the floor of the pavilion. Stunned, the Dark Witch raised her head and looked toward the fairies on the table.

The Light Witch laughed cruelly, advancing toward her rival. "They cannot help you," she sneered. "I have their wands. They are helpless."

Luna could wait no longer to take action. "Wrong," she said, in answer to the Light Witch's statement. But she said this very quietly so the Light Witch could not hear, adding, "We are not helpless." Then she told her friends, "Move away from the walls of the box."

The fairies moved backwards very quickly while Luna placed her hands flat against the walls of the box of light and very softly uttered, "*Break*." Instantly, the box shattered and the fairies were freed.

Luna wasted no time expressing any relief that the spell had worked properly. She flew directly to the Light Witch, who had turned toward the fairies, startled by the sound of the box breaking. Very quickly, Luna raised her hands. Glittering blue light shot out of her palms at the Light Witch. The force of the beams of light energy pushed the evil witch up against one of the stone pillars.

The Light Witch struggled but could not free herself, and there was an intense look of shock on her face. Clearly, she had discounted any further fairy action.

The Dark Witch had regained some of her strength. She stood beside the fairies in front of the Light Witch. With a few soft words in a language that the fairies could not understand, the Dark Witch spoke to the Light Witch. The force of her words drew the evil woman, struggling and screaming, toward the mirror. And with a slight wave of the Dark Witch's hand, the Light Witch was sucked into the mirror, where she fell instantly into a deep sleep on the couch, imprisoned by the same spell that had previously trapped the Dark Witch.

As she turned to face the fairies, the Dark Witch waved her hand again. With the wave, the remaining two boxes of light vanished, freeing the elf owl and the bat fairies. Warmth flooded into the pavilion, and the fairies no longer felt cold.

The Dark Witch smiled kindly at the fairies. Her expression was full of happiness and light, and she was many times more beautiful than the Light Witch. The fairies couldn't understand why they hadn't noticed this right away, and it was hard to fathom why it had taken them so long to recognize evil.

Next, the Dark Witch produced the fairies' wands from her own pocket, where she had magically placed them while casting the spell to imprison the Light Witch. Then she carefully returned the wands to their owners, winking at Luna as she handed her the cactus thorn.

With yet another wave of her hand, the Dark Witch miniaturized the grand piano down to the size of a pea. And with a further flick of her finger, the teeny piano sailed into the Dark Witch's pocket. It was

very unlikely that anyone would be able to take the piano from her, and even less likely that anyone could play the song needed to release the Light Witch correctly on such a small instrument.

The Dark Witch then conjured up food and water on the table for the fairies and sat down with them while they ate to regain their strength.

Chapter Seven

The Dark Witch's Story

Whit's Story

When the Dark Witch finally spoke to them, her soft voice was full of kindness. "It is a good thing for me that fairies are clever, and not easily deceived."

The fairies did not feel worthy of any praise or gratitude. They all felt it had taken them far too long to realize they were being misled.

The Dark Witch seemed to sense their frustration with themselves because she said, "Do not feel badly about being taken in by her. She is brilliant, as well as evil."

The tiny elf owl flew to the Dark Witch and landed on her shoulder. He nuzzled her neck, hooting softly. The two were obviously friends. The sphilox changed back into ladybug form and came to rest on the witch's other shoulder.

"While you eat and rest, I'll tell you my story," said the Dark Witch. "Then I will accompany you to Madam Toad's house. I would like to speak to her, anyway. I will also safely carry the bat fairies to their homes."

The fairies made themselves comfortable, eating and drinking while they listened.

"First," began the witch, "I need to tell you that I am the most powerful Dark Witch born in a century. But you have nothing to fear from me. It is true that the magic I possess is dark magic, but I never use it for evil. That is my choice.

"I was initially created by the Demon of Darkness, using a spell that could only be used one time." The Dark Witch paused for a moment, then quietly continued. "I was born dark and dangerous, and on the brink of becoming one of the most terrible evil forces the world has ever known. However, no creature that contains life is ever pure evil, or entirely bad, because life itself is good. There is always some small goodness, even in dark beings. The good inside me is in the form of a tiny light, only a pinprick, no bigger than a grain of sand." The Dark Witch glanced at the ladybug on her shoulder as she went on. "But small things can be very powerful. The light in me may be miniscule in size, but it is very strong.

"As a very young child, I was given a single chance for a different life. In a fleeting moment, two choices were placed before me. One was the option to follow

the path into darkness. The dark path would have been a very smooth one, full of comfort and ease for me, since it was my intended purpose in life. My second option was to cling to the tiny light inside me, and allow the light to battle the darkness in me for the rest of my life. I chose this path—the path of light. I live a life of pain with the battle that ever rages inside me. But it is nothing compared to the pain I could have inflicted on other creatures of the earth had I chosen the dark path."

The Dark Witch looked very solemn as she continued her story. "Even now, if I were to let go of the light and allow darkness to take over, I would be an unstoppable evil force. But there is no danger of that," she added, smiling softly. "I stand by my choice, and I am always in control. I will never serve the Demon of Darkness."

Suddenly, the Dark Witch's story was interrupted by the sound of four gorfenklugs rapidly approaching the pavilion. The ground shook with their pounding footsteps. The fairies all gasped in fear at the sight of the advancing beasts.

The Dark Witch stood up, and Snapdragon flew to hover near her shoulder. The look on Snapdragon's face was very determined, as she held her wand high, preparing to defend everyone against the approaching monsters. The boar bristle itself snorted slightly in preparation for use, if necessary.

The Dark Witch grinned as she spoke to Snapdragon. "There will be no need for that. The gorfenklugs are under the direction of the Light Witch, and she is currently unavailable to command them. They will not dare approach us too closely because they fear my power." As she walked to the edge of the pavilion to show herself

GORFENKLUG

to the gorfenklugs, the Dark Witch smiled somewhat mischievously, and added, "Actually, it will be very interesting if they do decide to face me."

The air was tingling with intensity, as they waited. But the Dark Witch was right. When the gorfenklugs saw that she was free from the mirror, with the Light Witch nowhere in sight, they hesitated only slightly before turning and breaking into a run in their haste to return to the safety of the black lake.

When the Dark Witch and Snapdragon had made their way back to the table, the Dark Witch spoke reassuringly to the fairies. "Even though we are currently in the Land of Darkness, you need not fear the Demon of Darkness. He is not very powerful. In fact, without evil agents like the Light Witch to do his bidding, he is virtually helpless. And many people have less to fear from darkness than they suppose.

"The Light Witch was also given a choice as a child. But she chose to take the path into darkness and become a servant of the Demon of Darkness. It is very sad that she chose to do what was easy, instead of what was right. She will be bound to serve the demon for the rest of her life because her choice created a bond that cannot be broken.

"I think you will enjoy the next part of my story," the Dark Witch said, smiling, her dark eyes twinkling. "I know Madam Robin very well. I was the one who gave her the gift of speech and long life. I am pleased that she chose to keep the gift and direct some of her energies into mentoring young fairies."

The fairies were all surprised to learn about Madam Robin's enchantment, and they listened intently as the Dark Witch went on. "Madam Robin was present at the very moment I was given my choice as a child. Seeing a beautiful songbird at the instant the two paths were laid before me influenced me toward the way of good, rather than evil. I have Madam Robin to thank for helping me to make the right decision.

"However, there is more to the struggle than what I have told you. The Demon of Darkness was thwarted by my choice, since he used up the one-time magic to create me. Since the moment I defied him, he has held an intense grudge born of his anger with my decision. He is always scheming, hoping to trick me into converting to darkness. On his instructions, the Light Witch constantly pursues me. It is the demon's hope that I will someday kill the Light Witch during one of our confrontations."

The Dark Witch's voice lowered as she explained. "If I were to ever kill another creature, the action would extinguish the light inside me that I ever cling to. I would be thrown into darkness and would be forced to serve the demon with my terrible power. And my service would be much more useful to him than that of the Light Witch, since I would then be fulfilling my intended purpose.

"This is the reason I keep council with the elves, the oldest and wisest of all magical creatures, and why the sphilox is willing to help me. Elves and sphiloxes cannot be corrupted or used for dark purposes.

"I am forever on my guard," the Dark Witch added, as she ruffled the feathers of the tiny owl nestled on her shoulder, still nuzzling at her neck. "When I pursued the Light Witch into the well two days ago to try to rescue the bat fairies, she had readied a trap for me. A *Containment Spell* was already in place, waiting for me. The only way I could have avoided the spell that trapped me in the mirror would have been to kill the Light Witch, thus canceling her magic in progress.

"But she knows I cannot kill, so she knew that she had me. The Light Witch has a bitterness born in her because of the demon's desire that she act as a sacrifice to convert me to evil. She, of course, would prefer to kill *me*. That is *her* intent with each of our encounters."

The fairies were all listening carefully to the witch's story and were very interested. When the Dark Witch took a little break from talking to have a drink of water, the local fairies silently offered some of their lemon jellybeans to the bat fairies. The spotted bat fairy was overjoyed. She loved lemon jellybeans, like all fairies in North America. However, the British and Thai fairies both looked confused. Apparently, they had never had lemon jellybeans. But they accepted them gladly, smiling and thanking their new friends.

The British fairy spoke English so the local fairies were able to understand her. However, they couldn't understand the language of the fairy from Thailand, so they just smiled and nodded politely at her words of thanks.

The Dark Witch finished drinking and started again with her story. "There is no legend about bat fairies being more powerful than other fairies. The Light Witch cleverly thought that up as part of the trap because she knew other fairies would try to rescue them. She started a rumor that I had kidnapped the fairies, and she needed an excuse when blaming me for their abduction as to why bat fairies were chosen."

The Dark Witch's tone became more serious as she went on. "The weakness of the Demon of Darkness lies in his beliefs and ideals. He often focuses on power, ignoring will. Will is much stronger. It doesn't matter how much power one possesses. It is the choices we make of how we use power that make us either weak or strong. True strength is a combination of wisdom and will, not power."

The Dark Witch sighed a little wearily as she continued. "The Light Witch is actually more powerful than I am." She nodded as the fairies' eyes widened in surprise. "And using light magic for dark purposes can be very dangerous and deadly. Light magic is definitely more powerful than dark magic. However, her choice to use light magic improperly is her weakness. Light magic is not as effective used darkly. Likewise, using dark magic for good is not as potent as it would be if used for evil. So I do not have as much power because of my choice."

The Dark Witch gazed fondly at the bat fairies as she added, "The bat fairies are no more powerful than other fairies, but they are good, and strong."

Chapter Eight

Leaving the Well Behind

As she got up from the chair to get ready to take the fairies home, the Dark Witch said, "Don't worry, the Light Witch will not suffer the same fate she had planned for me. I will keep her trapped in the mirror for the time being, at least until she is not a danger to anyone, but I will make sure she has food and water. She will not starve, and she will be reasonably comfortable. Plus, it's always a good thing to get caught up on one's sleep."

The group then made their way to the upside down opening of the well, as the

Dark Witch told them, "I cannot perform the magic to take you home until we are outside of the well. It will not work in the Land of Darkness. We must be in our own world. Are you strong enough to fly, or should I carry you?" she asked.

The local fairies were all able to fly, but the bat fairies were still very tired. The Dark Witch gathered them gently in her hands and slipped into position under the rim of the well.

While the local fairies flew, the Dark Witch rose silently and magically beside them, higher and higher, until they were all clear of the Well of Secrets.

It was after midnight and very dark in the woods by the well. Firefly glowed as brightly as possible to provide light for them.

Once more, the Dark Witch spoke a strange language, casting a spell, while standing by the opening of the well and gazing into it. When she finished the spell, she told the fairies, "I have sealed the doorway again so others cannot enter easily. It was unsealed by the Light Witch. I will make sure she never has the opportunity to take innocent beings into Eventide again."

Then the Dark Witch spoke to the tiny owl on her shoulder. "And you, my friend, are the bravest owl that ever lived," she said, blowing lightly on his feathers. "No bird has ever dared come near the Well of Secrets, let alone, entered. Thank you for bringing the sphilox.

"Thank you all for coming to help," added the Dark Witch, smiling at the fairies.

Next, the witch instructed the fairies to sit along her outstretched arm and close their eyes. Then she magically transported them all to Madam Toad's house. The trip was instantaneous, similar to

an elf *Travel-Sleep Spell*, but the fairies stayed awake. They didn't have to sleep for forty-five minutes to come out of the spell like they would have had to with elf travel.

Madam Toad and Madam Robin were both awake. They had been waiting up, worried, and hoping for good news. Their faces wore looks of intense relief when the Dark Witch appeared out of thin air in Madam Toad's parlor holding the eight fairies.

"I knew! I knew!" cried Madam Robin in her beautiful song voice, addressing the Dark Witch. "I knew the rumors couldn't be true. I was sure you had done no wrong."

Chirping happily, Madam Robin flew to the Dark Witch's shoulder and landed next to the owl. The Dark Witch smiled and stroked Madam Robin's feathers affectionately.

Madam Toad also smiled and nodded. She was very relieved to have her fairies back safely. She had not believed the rumor either—that the Dark Witch had abducted the bat fairies with evil intent.

"I can't stay to talk right now," said the Dark Witch. "I need to return the bat fairies to their homes. And I am going to have to do some fancy magic to fix things," she added. "Since these three girls have been missing for two days, I'm sure there are many authorities and searchers involved in looking for them.

"I will return later to explain what has happened, since your own fairies are very tired and probably need to sleep, rather than embarking on long stories." With this, the Dark Witch disappeared with the bat fairies.

Even though the fairies were tired, they couldn't sleep or rest until they had thoroughly explained all of the events that had occurred. They told Madam Toad and Madam Robin everything—about the merfolk, the well, Eventide, the Light Witch, the mirror, the owl, the sphilox, the piano, the gorfenklugs, and the Dark Witch's story.

"The Dark Witch shared with us about your bewitchment, Madam Robin," Luna said. "But we won't tell anyone else because we want to keep your mystique alive." The other fairies all nodded and smiled.

Madam Robin chirped in agreement since it was a rather personal issue, and she liked the idea of being thought of as somewhat mysterious.

Finally, Luna added, "We also know not to say anything about this mission to other fairies. We all agree with you that the Well of Secrets should be kept secret. No good can come of anyone seeking it, or entering the doorway. Eventide truly is a horrible place."

On New Year's Eve, Luna sat on her bed reading a book. She had just returned home with her parents from a long  drive to view Christmas lights. The twinkling lights made her think about the tiny light inside the Dark Witch.

Luna felt sorry for the Dark Witch, with the painful struggle against the darkness always battling inside her. But she admired the Dark Witch very much. Luna had never been tempted to use her fairy gifts for ill. She strictly adhered to the rules and the Fairy Code of Conduct. However, she could imagine circumstances where one might be inspired or misguided into using power unwisely.

She always had a slight fear of this in the back of her mind because of her abilities. Luna knew it was no accident that Madam Toad had chosen her for this mission. Not only had her skills been useful; but also, meeting the Dark Witch and hearing her story further strengthened Luna's resolve to only use her gifts for good, when necessary, and with permission.

Luna knew she held a very unique fairy gift, and that her magic was possibly even stronger than Madam Toad's. As she thought about all of the things involved with her abilities, she realized that her worry was actually a good thing. Her fears didn't mean that she would ever do anything wrong. Rather, they were a guide for her to always be diligent and careful.

As Luna sat reading and thinking, her mother brought two small packages into her room that had arrived with the day's mail. One of the boxes was from Thailand and was full of cinnamon jellybeans. The

second box was from England and held toffee jellybeans.

No wonder the bat fairies had been confused by the lemon jellybeans. Apparently, cinnamon and toffee were the preferred fairy jellybean flavors in these other countries.

"Pen pals," Luna said, in answer to her mother's questioning look. "It was a Girls

Club activity. I chose girls from England and Thailand for pen pals."

Luna carefully cut the return addresses from the wrapping on the packages so that she could write to her new friends. Then she settled back on her pillow to continue reading while she ate some of the cinnamon and toffee jellybeans. They were very good, but nothing was better than lemon jellybeans.

The End

Fairy Fun

From the Fairy Handbook:

Preferred Fairy Jellybean Flavors in Various Countries

Fairies love to play a game called "If I were a jellybean, what flavor would I be?" The fairies living in North America are not allowed to pick lemon because that is the favorite flavor of all North American fairies. After choosing their flavor, the girls look in their handbooks to discover which fairies around the world prefer the same.

Africa—orange
Antigua—caramel corn
Argentina—butterscotch

Australia and New Zealand—mint

Austria—gingerbread

Barbados—green apple

Belgium—chocolate

Bonaire—pineapple

Brunei—peach

Canada, Mexico, and
* United States—lemon and lime*

Chile—cantaloupe

China—watermelon

Croatia—tea

Cuba—cherry

Ecuador—strawberry

Egypt—pomegranate

England, Scotland, and
* Wales—toffee*

Estonia—fruit punch

Finland—pistachio

Germany—apple strudel

Gibraltar—fudge

Greece—kiwi

Greenland—mincemeat

Grenada—cotton candy

Iceland—egg custard

India—honeydew

Israel—honey

Kenya—pear

Laos—root beer

Malta—chocolate éclair

Martinique—grape

Monaco—grapefruit

Morocco—cranberry

Nepal—vanilla

Netherlands—licorice

Norway—coconut

Panama—caramel apple

Russia—marzipan

Singapore—apricot

South Africa—praline cheesecake

Sweden—taffy

Thailand—cinnamon

Yemen—white chocolate

Tracking the Moon

The word "Luna" was the name of an ancient Roman goddess of the moon. As time went on, people used the word "lunar" to mean anything having to do with the moon, such as a lunar eclipse (which is when the earth's shadow blocks the light from the sun on the moon).

The moon goes through many phases during the year as it circles the earth. These phases are when we see different versions of the illuminated part of the moon from the earth. Sometimes the moon is full and the entire part that we can see is lit up. Other times the moon looks like a tiny sliver in the sky.

Try keeping track of what the moon looks like every day for a month. You may ask an adult if you can draw on a calendar page or create your own blank calendar grid. To make your own calendar grid, you will need a ruler, a piece of paper, and a pencil or pen. You will need to draw enough boxes on your paper to have one box for each day of the month. Start out by using your ruler to draw eight vertical lines spaced about an inch apart. Then on top of those lines, draw seven horizontal lines spaced about an inch apart. You should now have seven vertical columns and six horizontal rows. Write each day of the week across the top of the columns. Then number the days of the month for the one you are working on.

When it is dark outside, look for the moon. In the correct box for that day, draw what you see. Is it big and bright? Is it skinny and hard to see? If it is too cloudy to see the moon, make a note on your chart.

Can you predict what the moon will look like before the next time you see it? How much do you think it will change from day to day?

Elf Owls

At five inches high, elf owls are the smallest of all owls. They mainly live in the Southern United States and Mexico. Elf owls like to nest in abandoned woodpecker holes in trees and cacti. They hatch three chicks at a time, called owlets, and the young are generally ready to set out on their own within a month. Elf owls mainly eat insects and are very good at chasing down flying insects. They have also been known to eat scorpions by somehow managing to pinch off their stingers.

Ladybugs

Ladybugs are insects that many people admire because of their brightly colored bodies. Although the red and black colors attract humans, they are a warning sign to predators that they should not eat the ladybugs! Ladybugs are able to emit a bad smell and taste when they are being threatened; if a bird tries to eat one, it will not taste very good. The bright red colors of the insect act as a reminder and help keep the ladybug safe.

Farmers are especially fond of ladybug beetles because they actually help keep pests out of their crops! Aphids are a plant-eating insect that can often destroy many of the plants farmers are growing. Ladybugs feed on the aphids, saving the farmers' crops. Many people believe ladybugs are a sign of good luck. This belief probably began when farmers realized that the beetles were helping to keep bad bugs out of the garden.

Luna Moths

Luna moths are only seen at night and it is a special treat if you are able to catch a glimpse of one. This moth's wings are a pale green color with large spots and long, curving tails at the ends. Their wingspan can be up to five inches wide, making this one of the largest moths in North America. They are commonly found in the eastern parts of the United States, but can be seen in other states as far west as Texas.

After hatching from an egg, the Luna moth begins its life as a caterpillar. The caterpillar enjoys eating a variety of tree leaves. This stage lasts for about three to four weeks and then it begins to spin its cocoon. It stays within the cocoon for two to three weeks as it goes through its metamorphosis to become a moth.

When the moth emerges from the cocoon, it is not yet ready to fly. The wings take several hours to fully spread out and dry. The moth will climb to a safe spot where its wings will be protected while they are drying. Once the wings are ready, the Luna moth will patiently wait until after dark to begin its adventure in the world. But its lifespan is only seven days long!

Bats

The bat fairies had fairy spirits of several very interesting types of bats:

Bumblebee bats are the world's smallest bats. They are about the same size as a large bumblebee and weigh about as much as a dime. Bumblebee bats are only found in a small area in western Thailand.

Pipistrelle bats are the smallest bats found in the United Kingdom. They like to live in areas such as parks, forests, farms, and even in cities. They especially love to eat insects. In fact, a single pipistrelle bat can eat up to 3,000 insects in one night!

Spotted bats are a very rare type of bat. They live in deserts and rocky areas in western North America, but they are hard to find. They have very large ears (the biggest of any North American bat) that are almost as big as their entire bodies!

Inside you is the power to do anything

The Fairy Chronicles

. . . the adventures continue

Cinnabar and the Island of Shadows

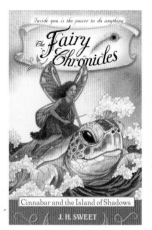

A shadow is a person's closest companion. Shadows protect and guide the humans they are attached to. But what if you were born without a shadow?

Madam Toad paused before she continued. "Human shadows are unlike any other shadows on earth. They are much different from animal, mountain, plant, cloud, insect, and building shadows. For starters, human shadows are much more complex. And they are the only shadows that are magically constructed. Human shadows are manufactured by shadowmakers on the Island of Shadows, and are delivered to children shortly after their births by hawks that work for the shadowmakers."

"Today, Mother Nature has discovered that seven children in various countries of the world have not received their shadows."

And so Cinnabar, Mimosa, Dewberry, and Spiderwort must travel to the Island of Shadows, confront the King and Queen of that remarkable place, discover what happened to these seven shadows, and, worst of all, find out if there might be someone or something behind it all!

Come visit us at fairychronicles.com

Mimosa and the River of Wisdom

Life is full of difficult choices. One of the hardest is having the power to help someone you love and not being able to. In such a situation, what would you do?

As they sat on the bed together, Mimosa sighed and tried to word her thoughts carefully. Periwinkle pulled her long dark hair back into a ponytail, clasping it with a stretchy hair tie, as she watched her friend's face closely, waiting for her to speak.

After a few moments, Mimosa sighed again, then finally said, "I'm really worried about my mom. She has tried so hard to quit smoking, but she can't. I want to help her."

"What do you mean, help her?" asked Periwinkle hesitantly.

"Well…" said Mimosa. "You know…a little fairy help."

"But you can't!" Periwinkle cried loudly. She glanced at the door and lowered her voice. "You know that we can't use fairy magic to solve personal problems. You could lose your fairy spirit."

Mimosa is one of the kindest, most courageous fairies in the world. But this is the hardest choice she has ever had to make. Should she use magic to help her mom even if it is forbidden? Should she risk losing her fairy spirit to do this?

Come visit us at fairychronicles.com

Primrose and the Magic Snowglobe

Burchard the gargoyle has just been fired from his job guarding a church from evil spirits because he can't stop walking around, Ripper the gremlin is fixing things instead of breaking them, and Mr. Jones the dwarf is telling people his own name and spreading dwarf secrets to non-dwarves. What is wrong with these people?

When Madam Toad had everyone's attention, she spoke more solemnly. "By now, many of you may have guessed why our visitors are here. It is unusual for a gargoyle to move around, for a gremlin to enjoy fixing things, and for a dwarf to reveal secrets. As far as anyone can tell, these are recent and singular occurrences among gargoyles, gremlins, and dwarves. Burchard has been fired from his job. Ripper has been driven out and is being pursued by other gremlins. And Mr. Jones has been banished by the dwarves.

"We have no idea how these things occurred," Madam Toad continued, "and a reason why must be found so that things can be put to right."

Primrose, Luna, and Snapdragon are put on the case, with the help of Madam Swallowtail. Interestingly, all three of the magical creatures remember making a wish and seeing a man with a snowglobe. Could it really be that the Wishmaker has returned? Primrose must use her detective abilities to solve the mystery.

Come visit us at fairychronicles.com

Dewberry and the Lost Chest of Paragon

In Dewberry's constant quest to obtain more knowledge, she uncovers the Legend of Paragon, an ancient ruler, and his three marshals— Exemplar, Criterion, and Apotheosis. Dewberry enlists the aid of her friends, Primrose and Snapdragon, in seeking the Lost Chest of Paragon, rumored to contain a great gift of ancient and powerful knowledge, one she hopes to share with all of mankind.

But when the chest is found, a catastrophe occurs, one so powerful that even fairy magic is nowhere near strong enough to fix the problem. But it was Dewberry's relentless search for knowledge that caused this disaster in the first place. She will have to do everything she can to make it right again...

 116

Moonflower and the Pearl of Paramour

Henry, a brownie prince, loves the fairy named Rose. Forty years ago, a bitter wizard cursed them to be forever apart and forever silent. Rose is trapped in a magic painting and Henry is trapped in a book. Neither can leave their prisons, nor speak a single word, or the other will die.

But every seventy-two years, the Wishing Star of Love appears for nine days only, and when wished upon, it can lead the wisher to Paramour, the Goddess of Love. With the help of the Goddess's magic pearl, there is a way to set the cursed couple free. Since Moonflower is the Fairy of Love, she will lead the mission to rescue Henry and Rose. Can Moonflower and her friends reach Henry and Rose in time or will the couple be imprisoned forever?

The adventures
don't end here!

Come visit us at
www.fairychronicles.com

for even more
fairy magic
and fun!

- Become a Fairy Chronicles member
- Upload your own fairy drawings
- Read about all of the *Fairy Chronicles* adventures—and get sneak peeks of the next books
- Meet each fairy and learn more about your favorite characters
- Help protect Mother Nature with cool recycling activities and ideas
- Check out the online Fairy Handbook as well as trivia, recipes, poems, and crafts
- Download special bookmarks, computer graphics, and more free stuff
- Send your friends *Fairy Chronicles* e-cards

And much more!

About the Author

J.H. Sweet has always looked for the magic in the everyday. She has an imaginary dog named Jellybean Ebenezer Beast. Her hobbies include hiking, photography, knitting, and basketry. She also enjoys watching a variety of movies and sports. Her favorite superhero is her husband, with Silver Surfer coming in a close second. She loves many of the same things the fairies love, including live oak trees, mockingbirds, weathered terra-cotta, butterflies, bees, and cypress knees. In the fairy game of "If I were a jellybean, what flavor would I be?" she would be green apple. J.H. Sweet lives with her husband in South Texas and has a degree in English from Texas State University.

About the Illustrator

Ever since she was a little girl, Tara Larsen Chang has been captivated by intricate illustrations in fairy tales and children's books. Since earning her BFA in Illustration from Brigham Young University, her illustrations have appeared in numerous children's books and magazines. When she is not drawing and painting in her studio, she can be found working in her gardens to make sure that there are plenty of havens for visiting fairies.